Dear Parents:

Congratulations! Your child is taking the first steps on an exciting journey. The destination? Independent reading!

STEP INTO READING® will help your child get there. The program offers five steps to reading success. Each step includes fun stories and colorful art or photographs. In addition to original fiction and books with favorite characters, there are Step into Reading Non-Fiction Readers, Phonics Readers and Boxed Sets, Sticker Readers, and Comic Readers—a complete literacy program with something to interest every child.

Learning to Read, Step by Step!

Ready to Read   Preschool–Kindergarten
• big type and easy words • rhyme and rhythm • picture clues
For children who know the alphabet and are eager to begin reading.

Reading with Help   Preschool–Grade 1
• basic vocabulary • short sentences • simple stories
For children who recognize familiar words and sound out new words with help.

Reading on Your Own   Grades 1–3
• engaging characters • easy-to-follow plots • popular topics
For children who are ready to read on their own.

Reading Paragraphs   Grades 2–3
• challenging vocabulary • short paragraphs • exciting stories
For newly independent readers who read simple sentences with confidence.

Ready for Chapters   Grades 2–4
• chapters • longer paragraphs • full-color art
For children who want to take the plunge into chapter books but still like colorful pictures.

STEP INTO READING® is designed to give every child a successful reading experience. The grade levels are only guides; children will progress through the steps at their own speed, developing confidence in their reading.

Remember, a lifetime love of reading starts with a single step!

DREAMWORKS

Trolls

Troll-tastic Tales

Step into Reading, Random House, and the Random House colophon are registered trademarks of Penguin Random House LLC.

Visit us on the Web!
StepIntoReading.com
rhcbooks.com

Educators and librarians, for a variety of tools, visit us at RHTeachersLibrarians.com

ISBN 978-0-593-12786-5

MANUFACTURED IN CHINA

10 9 8 7 6 5 4 3 2 1

DREAMWORKS

Trolls

Troll-tastic Tales

Step 2 and Step 3 Books
A Collection of Six Readers

Random House 🏠 New York

CONTENTS

DREAMWORKS

ALL ABOUT the TROLLS

by Kristen L. Depken

Random House 🏠 New York

Welcome to Troll Village!
It's the coolest place
to sing, dance,
and eat cupcakes!

There are friendly Trolls
of all shapes and sizes.
They all have awesome talents
and make Troll Village special.

This is Poppy!

She is the perky princess of Troll Village.

Poppy is bright and cheerful!

She loves to sing and dance.

She also loves to hug.

She hugs her friends

every hour on the hour!

Branch is gray and grumpy.

Branch is always worried.

He lives by himself

in a super-secret bunker.

Branch does not like
singing or dancing.
He is definitely *not* a hugger.

Cooper has pink striped fur.

He plays the harmonica
and loves to dance.

He is the most playful
Troll around.

Sweet Biggie is the biggest Troll
and has the biggest heart.
He is almost eight inches tall!
Biggie has a cute best friend
named Mr. Dinkles.
He loves to dress Mr. Dinkles
in cute outfits.

Satin and Chenille are fashion twins.

They are connected by their hair.

Satin is pink. Chenille is blue.

They make super-stylish outfits

for every Troll Village event.

They may look alike,

but they never dress alike!

DJ Suki is the Troll Village music mixer.
She brings her own music
to every party.

This is Guy Diamond!

He never wears any clothes

but is covered in glitter

from head to toe.

His glitter brings

a sparkle to any party!

Maddy works hair magic!

She runs the hair salon.

She helps every Troll

look amazing.

Creek is cool and calm.

He is a great yoga teacher,

a groovy dancer,

and a kind friend.

He always knows what to say

to cheer up the other Trolls.

Meet Fuzzbert!

He is hard to understand

through all that hair,

so the Trolls just have to guess

what he is saying.

Smidge is a tiny Troll

with a big voice.

She is very fit,

thanks to her favorite hobby—

lifting weights with her hair!

Harper loves to paint.

Her hair is the best paintbrush!

Paint flies everywhere

when she creates amazing art!

Karma loves camping,

climbing trees,

and playing with critters.

They love playing

in her garden of hair!

Cybil is the wisest troll

in Troll Village.

She is a great listener,

but her advice can be a little silly.

Not everyone is
as happy as the Trolls.
The Bergens are
unhappy creatures.

They think eating Trolls

will make them happy.

King Gristle is the king

of Bergen Town.

He wants to bring happiness

to his kingdom—with Trolls.

He can't wait to eat one!

Chef is a whiz in
the Bergen Town kitchen.
Her favorite Troll recipes
are Trollcakes
and Egg Trolls.

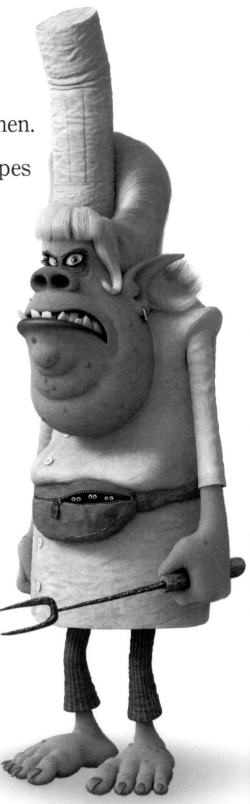

Bridget is a maid

in the kitchen of the castle.

She is sweet and kind.

No one pays attention to Bridget.

Then the Trolls give her

a makeover.

She becomes the fancy

Lady Glittersparkles!

Poppy and her friends teach
the silly Bergens how to be happy
without eating Trolls.

Poppy wants
everyone to share
their true colors!

POPPY'S PARTY

by Frank Berrios

illustrated by Fabio Laguna,
Gabriella Matta, and Francesco Legramandi

Random House New York

This is Troll Village.
It is the happiest place—
with the happiest trees
and the happiest creatures.
They are called Trolls.
It is also the place
Poppy calls home!

Poppy loves
to dance and sing.
She also loves
to sing and dance.
And today she gets to do both!
She is very excited.

Poppy is going to throw
the biggest, loudest,
craziest party ever!
King Peppy can't wait!

Everyone is getting ready
for Poppy's party.
But first Poppy has to
pass out the invitations!

Poppy's friend Smidge

is super small but super strong.

She gives Poppy a super lift!

Poppy brings Biggie
an invitation.

He is a big softie.

He cries happy tears.

Poppy visits Creek.

He always gives good advice,

and everyone hangs on

his every word.

Creek is a super-cool Troll.

Poppy knows that Guy Diamond

will make her party shine.

He shakes off a cloud

of glitter whenever he dances!

Poppy drops in to see the twins,
Satin and Chenille.

Poppy's fashionable friends
will create awesome dresses
for her to wear before, during,
and after the party!

Poppy practices
her dance moves with Cooper.
No one can dance like Cooper.
That's because he is
the only Troll with four feet!

DJ Suki is creating a special
playlist for Poppy's after-party.
DJ Suki uses all sorts of
critters to make music.
She is always ready
to drop the beat!

Poppy's friend Fuzzbert
loves to tickle the Trolls.
He is also a tickler
on the dance floor!

Branch is a very different Troll.

He does not like to sing.

He does not like to dance.

He does not like to sing

or dance or hug!

Poppy gives Branch
a special invitation.
She knows she can help him
find his true colors.
With a song in your heart,
you can do anything!

At the party, Smidge sends
glitter sparkles into the sky.
DJ Suki turns up the volume.
She makes it loud!

The Trolls sing and dance,
and hug and sing,
and dance and hug
at Poppy's biggest,
loudest, craziest
party ever!

Everything is rainbows
and cupcakes.
Hug Time!

DREAMWORKS

TROLLS

POPPY and BRANCH'S
BIG ADVENTURE

by Mona Miller

Random House 🏠 New York

I'm King Peppy.
This is the story
of how my daughter
became queen.

Her name is Poppy,

and she is the

happiest, singing-est Troll

in Troll Village.

Her friend Branch
was a gray Troll.
He did not like
to dance, sing,
or even hug!

He warned Poppy

to be quiet,

or our enemies,

the Bergens,

might hear.

Who are the Bergens?
The Bergens were once
unhappy giants
who lived in
Bergen Town.
They liked to groan
and complain.

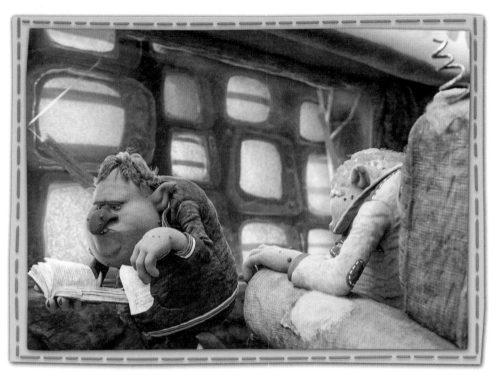

Worst of all, they thought
that eating Trolls
was the only thing
that would ever
make them happy.

When a Bergen named Chef
found Troll Village,
she took many
of Poppy's friends.

Poppy bravely set off
into the big, wide world
to find and save them!

Her journey was not easy.

There was beauty.

And there was also danger.

But Poppy never

gave up hope!

On the way, she was attacked
by big, fuzzy spiders!
Why does everyone
want to eat Trolls?

Poppy was wrapped
in a ball of spiderweb.
She seemed like a goner
for sure!

That was when Branch
finally showed up.
He rescued her
from the spiders!

Poppy always knew

Branch would come.

She thought they

made a great team.

Together they continued
through the forest.
It was a long trip.
Poppy talked about
her rescue plan.

Branch was willing

to help Poppy

save their friends . . .

. . . but he was not so sure

her plan would work.

Poppy had a way

of looking at things

on the bright side.

Branch only saw danger.

Poppy and Branch
eventually found
some tunnels that led
to Bergen Town.

But they did not know

which one to take.

They met a new friend
named Cloud Guy,
who offered to show them
the correct path.

He helped, but first
he teased Branch
by making him give
hugs and fist bumps.

Poppy and Branch
finally made it into
the Bergen castle—
only to be caught
by Chef!

Chef was going to cook

all the Trolls

for King Gristle!

For the first time ever,
Poppy lost all hope—
and all her color.
The other Trolls did, too.

They became gray, like Branch.

But then something

amazing happened.

Branch started to sing!

Poppy got her colors back,

and Branch wasn't gray anymore!

Then all the Trolls

became colorful again.

Singing had made

their true colors appear!

After that, Poppy and Branch
showed the Bergens
that there were better ways
to be happy than by
eating Trolls.

So we danced and sang
and made Poppy our queen!
But I bet our adventures
are just beginning!

DREAMWORKS

TROLLS

DROP the BEAT!

by David Lewman

illustrated by Fabio Laguna
and Gabriella Matta

Random House 🏠 New York

DJ Suki plays music.
It thumps and pumps
from her Wooferbug!

Biggie hears the music.
His pet, Mr. Dinkles,
bobs his head.
Biggie and Mr. Dinkles
love DJ Suki's music!

Biggie asks DJ Suki
what she is doing.
DJ Suki says she has
dropped the beat
on a new song!

That means she has
started the music,
but Biggie is confused.

Biggie thinks DJ Suki has *lost* her beat!

He and Mr. Dinkles

decide to find it

for her.

Biggie asks Cooper
if he has seen
DJ Suki's lost beat.

Cooper says no,

but he offers

to play his harmonica!

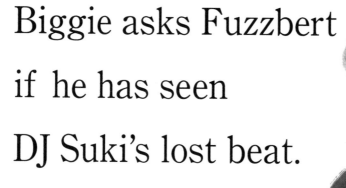

Biggie asks Fuzzbert
if he has seen
DJ Suki's lost beat.

Fuzzbert shakes his head.
Then he starts to hum
and whistle.
It sounds super
with Cooper's harmonica.

Biggie asks Guy Diamond
if he has seen
DJ Suki's lost beat.

Guy Diamond says no.

Then he starts to sing!

Biggie asks him

to come along.

Biggie asks
Satin and Chenille
if they have seen
DJ Suki's lost beat.

Satin and Chenille

say no.

But they can

sing harmony!

They will come along, too!

Biggie asks Poppy
if she has seen
DJ Suki's lost beat.

Poppy has not.

But she can play

her cowbell.

It sounds great!

DJ Suki loves
her friends' music.
She tells Biggie
that dropping the beat
just means starting
a new song!

She invites the Trolls
to add all their
wonderful sounds
to her music.

The Trolls play and sing
the new song together.
The music *rocks*!

More Trolls come
when they hear it.

The Trolls play,
dance, and sing
all night long!

STEP INTO READING®

DREAMWORKS

TROLLS

The Sound of Spring

by David Lewman

illustrated by Fabio Laguna

Random House 🏠 New York

It is a warm spring night
in Troll Village.
All the Trolls are sleeping,
except one.

Branch is wide awake.

He hears something.

What's that sound?

It sounds like chirping.
Is there a bird
in the house?

Branch looks around.

No bird!

In the morning,
Branch still hears
chirping.

He checks the village.
He cannot find
what is making
the sound.

The chirping is
driving him crazy!

Branch asks Cloud Guy
if he hears the sound.
Cloud Guy listens.

He hears
the chirping, too.
He asks Branch
if *he* is making the sound.

Branch says no.

Cloud Guy says

Branch *must*

be chirping!

Branch says,
"I am *not* chirping!"
Branch thinks Cloud Guy
is playing a trick on him.

He is angry.

He chases Cloud Guy

through the woods!

Poppy sees her friends.
She asks them
what's wrong.
Branch tells Poppy
about the chirping.

Poppy listens closely.
She knows where
the sound
is coming from!

Poppy reaches into
Branch's hair
and pulls out an egg!

That is where
the chirping
is coming from!
A bird must have laid
an egg in Branch's hair!

Poppy says the egg
is about to hatch!

A bird comes out
of the egg.
It sings a song.
Poppy and Branch
sing, too!

The little bird's
mother hears
her baby singing.
She comes right away!

They fly off together.

Everyone waves goodbye.
Branch misses the bird's
chirping a little . . .
but not *too* much.

DREAMWORKS

TROLLS

Color Day Party!

by Mary Man-Kong

illustrated by Fabio Laguna

Random House 🏠 New York

It is a busy day
in Troll Village.
Everyone is getting ready
for the Color Day party.
All the Trolls will wear
their favorite color.

There are so many
great colors!
Poppy does not know
which color to wear.

She decides to ask
her friends.

In Troll Village,
Poppy meets Cooper.
Cooper is going
to wear red.
He has an idea.

He gives Poppy
a red scarf.
Poppy loves red.
Maybe she will wear
red, too!

DJ Suki is going
to wear orange.
"I am rocking the orange,"
she says.

She gives Poppy
orange headphones.
Poppy loves orange.
Maybe she will wear
orange, too!

Smidge is going
to wear yellow.
"Yellow gives
me strength,"
she says.

She gives Poppy
a yellow bow.
Poppy loves yellow.
Maybe she will wear
yellow, too!

Fuzzbert is tickled
to be green.
His fuzzy hair
tickles Poppy!
Fuzzbert has an idea.

He gives Poppy
a green bracelet.
Poppy loves green.
Maybe she will wear
green, too!

Even Branch is going
to wear his favorite color.
He will wear blue.

He gives Poppy
a blue vest.
Poppy loves blue.
Maybe she will wear
blue, too!

Poppy visits
Satin and Chenille.
They are going
to wear indigo
and violet.

They give her
an indigo jumper
and violet leggings.
Poppy loves those colors.
Maybe she will wear
them, too!

When Poppy gets home,
she does not know
what to do.

She loves all
the different colors.
Suddenly,
Poppy has an idea.

At the Color Day party,
everyone wears
a different color.

But Poppy wears
all the colors!
She looks like a rainbow.
The Trolls love it!

Happy
Color Day!